Angel Whisper

Jazmine L. Swanson

Copyright © 2010 by Jazmine L. Swanson

Published by JLS BOOKS & MARKETING
P. O. Box 10583
Killeen, TX 76547

Contact us at:
st_murdocksw@yahoo.com

ISBN: 978-0-615-36922-8

Library of Congress Control Number: 2010909318

Printed in the United States of America

Acknowledgments

I want to give thanks to my family and God. Their support, patience, and encouragement, along with God's will, made it possible for me to publish my work and make my gift of writing known to the world. I also want to thank my friends and many new readers for their support. God bless everyone!

Chapter 1

The Meeting

"Wow! That party was awesome!" I proclaimed as Marina and I exited the teenage club onto the city streets.

"Hey, Jalissa, can you believe school is already about to start?"

"Time just seems to fly, huh?" I sighed and kicked a rock down the pavement.

"Yeah. Well, my mom is parked over there, so I will see you later."

Marina waved good-bye and entered her mother's car. I began my walk home, down the sidewalk and into the city night. I looked up into the sky and stared at the full moon above the skyscrapers.

"Man, that would be so cool if I could go to the moon," I announced aloud.

"Man, I see the full moon every day where I'm from," an unfamiliar male voice mocked.

I was startled by the response, and I turned to see a

homeless guy with light brown, spiked, darkly streaked hair sitting relaxed against an alley wall. His clothes were tattered, and I could barely see his face in the darkness. Feeling unthreatened, I ignored him. I continued to walk a few more feet when I saw the same guy standing in my periphery and pointing at the moon.

"Watch this!" exclaimed the homeless guy as he flew into the sky. He pinched his fingers together like he was holding a pencil and began moving an imaginary pencil over the moon. "Voila!"

Somehow, he had drawn funny faces on the moon. I stopped and rubbed my eyes. I had to make sure I was not daydreaming or seeing imaginary things. It was not unusual for me to zone out. After I rubbed my eyes, I realized he was still there. Suddenly, his appearance transformed to that of an average looking teenager. He had a tan complexion with hazel, almond-shaped eyes. I convinced myself this guy was not human … at all. Then I saw a white ray of light silhouette his body. I felt a soothing, warm, peaceful, positive presence emanating from him.

"I don't have any money for you, homeless guy … or whoever you are," I said sarcastically.

He tilted his head at me a little and smiled.

"I wasn't asking for money, party girl," he retorted playfully.

He had a sense of humor—I was intrigued.

"I don't know what you are, but I'm going home," I replied.

He drifted down from the sky and walked next to me.

"Who does this guy think he is?" I wondered.

"I'm going home, too!" replied the mysterious guy.

"Whatever."

He disappeared.

* * *

I turned the block, walked into my apartment complex, and walked up the stairs to my apartment. I opened the door and greeted my mother before I realized she was snoring on the couch. I shrugged and went into my room. I walked over to my window and adjusted my Venus flytrap on the windowsill.

Out of the corner of my eye, I saw that guy from earlier. This time, he was wearing scuba diving gear and swimming in the air above the street as he pretended to wrestle a shark. I sighed and rubbed my eyes again to make sure I was not hallucinating. I looked again, and yes, he was still swimming in the air wrestling a shark. This was so hard to believe, but I figured if I continued to ignore him, he would probably keep trying these drastic measures to get my attention. I waved at him. He stopped wrestling the shark, disappeared, and then appeared in my room with his scuba diving gear on.

"Who are you?"

"Em Deechay!" he exclaimed with his snorkel still on.

"Um, I can't understand you. Can you take that thing off?" I asked. The snorkel disappeared from his mouth.

"I'm TJ!" he exclaimed.

I rubbed my head. "That's nice. What are you?"

"Um, I'm not quite sure what my ethnicity is, I'm—"

His evasiveness frustrated me. "Hey! Are you a ghost? Monster? What?"

"Oh! My preference, um hum?" His apparel changed abruptly. He was now wearing reading glasses and a business suit. He started pulling out a bunch of papers from a suitcase.

"Hey," I said, "can you answer a simple question without being so dramatic?"

TJ took off his reading glasses and folded them. "Well excuse me, girlfriend," he said, snapping his fingers at me. "I'm anything you want me to be."

I rolled my eyes and turned my back on him.

"Well, you're a monster to me." I turned and looked at TJ. This time, he was wearing a purple, polyester Barney the dinosaur costume. I nearly died of laughter when I saw him.

"Do you think I'm scary, Jalissa?" he asked, giggling like Barney. "I think a lot of kids are afraid of that purple dinosaur."

He transformed back to his normal self.

"Okay, if you're not a monster, you have to be a zombie."

On cue, he magically wrapped himself in mummy clothes and walked around my room with both of his arms out in front of his body.

"I can't see a thing," he said as he bumped into the wall and fell down. I giggled with my hand over my mouth.

"Really, what are you?" I asked again, hoping to get a logical answer. TJ got up from the ground and transformed back to more normal clothing.

"Do you really want to know?" he asked.

"Um, yes!" I exclaimed.

"I'm an angel."

I gasped.

"What? You? No Way!" I said, snickering.

TJ gasped.

"You don't think I have what it takes to be an angel?" He pretended to cry.

"Um, well, I thought angels were supposed to be all holy and protective," I explained.

TJ stopped his whimpering and scratched his head. "Protect, yes. Holy, well, that's a different story. I'm holy enough."

"You're not one of those angels pictured in churches. Where are your wings?"

"Well, I'm not your traditional angel," he said with a French accent. "And who said angels had to have wings?"

"I see that. Well, bug me later, because I'm exhausted."

"If that's what you call it," TJ said in a sarcastic tone and disappeared. I doubted he was gone for good. I was a little dazed after my crazy encounter with TJ, so I prepared for bed. I brushed my teeth, slipped on my pajamas, turned the light off, and tucked myself in bed.

The next morning, I awakened to the peaceful chirping of birds outside of my bedroom window. I opened my eyes and turned to look out the window to see the birds. Unfortunately, there were no birds; TJ was the bird. I rolled my eyes and turned the other way in my bed. TJ popped into my room with a somber look on his face.

"You didn't think my singing was beautiful?" TJ asked, sniffling in a playful way.

I put my pillow over my head. "I don't like birds like you," I said. "Why are you stalking me?"

TJ gasped. "Stalking is such a negative way to put it. It's more like watching over you."

"Uh huh, is that right?"

"If you have a problem, you can take it up with … *him!*"

"Well, I might just do that then." I got out of bed and fixed my hair. It was quiet for a moment, but as usual, TJ began running his mouth. He clasped his hands together and pretended to look at a watch on his wrist.

"Are you still talking to *him*?" TJ questioned with a frightened tone. He assumed I was talking to God.

"Um, yeah, I guess." I packed my luggage and pre-pared to go to my grandma's place.

"No wonder none of the angels wanted to watch over you," TJ said. I gasped loudly. TJ continued, "Geez, what's your problem? You nearly gave me a heart attack."

"What do you mean nobody wanted to watch over me?" I asked.

"Nothing," TJ said.

"No, you better tell me!"

"Or what? You're gonna kill me or something? I'm already kind of ... not human," TJ said.

"Huhhh!" I shouted.

"Whoa, easy there, tiger," TJ said, trying to calm me. "I'm going to explain. You see, I was assigned to you according to your personality." He paused as if he was thinking of the correct words to use. "Well, your per-sonality is, uh, tough. You see, God assigned me to you because we're like total opposites. God was experiment-ing with different personalities and how they react." His expression displayed pride in his choice of words. "God's got a sense of humor, doesn't he?" said TJ.

"Can you finish?" I said.

"Well, we couldn't find any angels who were your opposite, except me of course. I was one of a kind," bragged TJ.

"My personality's tough? Are you sure you have the right person?"

"Well, let's see," TJ said, looking at his palm like he was reading from it. "Jalissa Saltz, sixteen years old, going into the eleventh grade, tan complexion, curly, black hair that hangs all the way to the middle of her back, and how would you describe them, sophisticated dark eyes?" He looked up at me, "That's you, isn't it?"

"Okay, so what are you suppose to do?"

"You know, watch over you, protect you, give you advice, make you laugh, and all that other angel stuff."

"So angels are supposed to be comedians now?" I asked, puzzled.

"Um, no, not really, that's just how I am. I'm a one-of-a-kind package deal," he said with a Southern accent.

I managed a slight grin. *How strange was this?*

"So, like, can other people see you?"

"Nope."

I nodded as I sat on my bed with an expression like I had received terrifying news. Suddenly, I did not feel normal anymore.

"Does this happen to everybody?"

"Not really, not a lot of people are deeply in tune with their spirituality."

"Oh, well I have to go to my grandma's house today," I said. "She stays out in the country, kind of in the middle of the woods. I'm going to crash at her place for the rest of the summer."

"Oh, I want to go with you!" he said.

"Well, I guess I have no choice," I said, shrugging. TJ disappeared from my room. I finished packing the last of my belongings, and my mom and I left to go to my grandma's place.

* * *

I rode in the backseat and listened to my iPod. Nearly an hour had passed, and I could not wait for the last thirty minutes of this trip to come to an end. To bide my time, I gazed out of the window at the trees while my mother drove deeper and deeper into the woods. I pondered seeing the lake behind my grandmother's house and visiting the hidden spring in the woods. I thought of how I would explore the woods when my grandmother was away.

"Mmph, mmph, mmph, somebody is being put on the naughty list for Christmas," said TJ as he appeared next to me in the backseat. "Here I was, thinking you were an angel."

I stared at him with a dismayed expression.

My mother looked at me in the rearview mirror.

"Honey, are you okay?" my mom asked.

"Um, yeah," I said and attempted to look normal again. TJ's bad timing was unbelievable.

"Why are you in my business anyway?" I whispered to TJ.

"Um, hello," TJ said. "I'm your angel."

"Honey, who are you talking to back there?" Mom asked.

"I'm not talking to anybody," I replied. "I'm just singing this song on my iPod."

"Liar, liar, liar, you're a liar," TJ whispered teasingly as he giggled. I mugged at him spitefully and turned to face the window. *This last couple weeks of the summer is going to be interesting*, I thought.

We finally arrived at my grandmother's cabin. I retrieved my luggage from the trunk of my mom's car. My mother kissed me good-bye and left for her business trip.

"Hey, Lissa," my grandmother greeted me. "I have your room ready for you. Come on in." I dragged my luggage full of clothes and accessories into her lodge. She escorted me to a bright pink room. My stuffed animals were still there from when I last visited her six years ago. My juvenile paintings of stick figures still hung on the walls.

"I'm going out to town, so I will be back in a few hours," my grandma said as she exited my room. TJ popped into my room and sat on my bed as I unpacked my summer clothes.

"You should go to the lake," TJ said. I gave him a puzzled stare.

"Aren't you the one that didn't want me to go? I

thought you were an angel?" I asked as I sort of choked on my words.

"I am; I'm just adventurous," TJ replied.

"Well," I said, "I was going to go anyway."

"So what are ya waiting for? Your grandma will be back soon," TJ said. I stared at him, grabbed my swim-suit, and left my grandma's cabin. TJ appeared next to me wearing hiking gear.

"Which way is it?" TJ asked with a smile.

"You're coming?" I asked.

"Um, yeah, I got to protect you if you get attacked by something, geez!" he said as he stomped toward the lake. I sighed and followed him. Surprisingly, our walk to the lake was filled with silence—at least until I asked him more about himself.

"So do you like what you do?" I said.

He stopped walking. In response, I stopped too. I was kind of startled; maybe I should not have asked him that. He finally turned back to me with a big smile. He looked around with squinted eyes and pointed at himself.

"Are you talking to me?" he asked.

I squinted at him and sighed.

"TJ, there is nobody else out here besides us," I said. "Of course I'm talking to you."

"I know," he said. He lifted his head and smiled again. "Actually, I love what I do."

I was a bit surprised. "W-Why?" I said.

"W-Why, you ask? I like being on earth. Luckily for me, I don't have to deal with all the responsibilities you humans have to deal with. I'm free! Sort of."

"I have always wondered what it would be like without responsibilities, to be free."

"Really, why is that?" TJ asked. I was shocked to see he had not made a silly impression or gotten on my nerves—he was actually listening.

"I've never really liked how the world works, how people hurt each other, and how selfish people can really be," I said. "There are not too many good people left in this world, and it makes me afraid sometimes … for our human race."

TJ clapped.

"Bravo, bravo, hmm … *He* was right about you. You're no average, rinky-dink teenager."

"What do you mean rinky-dink teenager, and why do you call God *him*?"

"In my dictionary, a rinky-dink teenager is one that is engaged in reckless behavior, is oblivious, and is ignorant to deep intellectual thought. They are very shallow human beings, I must say," TJ explained. "Also, I call God *him* because I'm cool like that."

"Well, you're kind of conceited to be an angel."

TJ gasped. "Well, you're not a normal teenager!" he said and stuck his tongue out at me.

I rolled my eyes. "I'm not the one who acts childish."

"Well, I'm not the one with a stick up my behind!"

I gasped. "No you didn't!"

"Yes I did, girlfriend, and there's plenty where that came from," said TJ while he bobbed his head and snapped his fingers. I stood there with an irritated expression on my face. I noticed we were near a cliff overlooking the lake. A sneaky grin crept across my face, but I changed it and did my best to look terrified.

"Hey! TJ look!" I shouted. "There's a shark in the lake!" TJ ran up to the edge of the cliff and looked down at the lake. I crept up behind him and pushed him off the cliff into the lake.

Splash!

"Ha ha ha! Who's the one with the stick up their behind now!" I yelled. TJ swam up to the surface of the water.

"Hey!" shouted TJ as he swam on his back, "sharks don't live in freshwater!" I watched him from the cliff. "C'mon in," he shouted. "Uh-oh, I forgot I have your swimsuit!" TJ held up my pink, polka dot swimsuit. "Ha ha, now you can't get into the water!"

"Yes, I can!" I jumped off the cliff and splashed into the lake fully clothed. After I swam around a little bit, I floated on my back and bathed in the summer air. I turned my head and saw TJ submerged. He surfaced wearing my swimsuit over his clothes.

He swam around and asked, "Don't I look cute and

sassy?" Then he paused and asked, "Hey, why aren't you allowed to go to this lake?"

"My grandma says there's a myth that spirits roam this lake. I think it's a bunch of crap," I said, brushing off the topic.

"She's right, I can see them," TJ said. "Don't worry, they're harmless." TJ calmly lifted himself out the water onto the shore. "C'mon, let's hurry and beat your grandma home." I nodded and got out of the water. My clothes were soaking wet. TJ shook himself off like a puppy, and he was fully dry.

"Aw, looks like somebody is all wet," TJ said. "Too bad, so sad. It's payback for pushing me off the cliff." TJ smiled and walked toward my grandma's cabin, but then he stopped and turned around. "Nah, I wouldn't do that to you." He touched my shoulder, and somehow I was dry.

We made it back to my grandma's cabin in no time. Five minutes later, my grandma arrived home.

"Sorry I'm late, Lissa, I just picked up some groceries from town," she explained. "I bought you some fresh chocolate strawberries. Help yourself." Then she retreated to her room.

I happily opened my pack of strawberries and turned to see TJ staring at me with a sad, puppy-face expression. I giggled. He looked so cute, just like a puppy.

"Here, you can have some strawberries." I handed him two of the big ones.

"For me? Aw thanks," said TJ as he gracefully ate the strawberries. I turned to face the window and saw that it was nightfall. I walked to my room and settled myself. After I showered and put on my pajamas, I picked out my clothes for the next day.

TJ popped into my room. "So, what's planned for tomorrow?" He wore a green face-mask with his hair wrapped in a towel. I could not help but laugh.

"I don't know," I said. "You figure something out. Goodnight." I yawned, stretched out on my bed, and quickly fell asleep.

Chapter 2

Spirit of the Lake

I heard a rooster crow in my room. Startled, I looked, only to find TJ doing a rooster impression. I looked out the window to see it was still dark outside. I rolled my eyes at him.

"What's your problem? It's still dark outside!"

"It's six in the morning, and I'm bored, so let's go," demanded TJ.

"What, uh, no. I can't leave."

"Why not? You scared you'll get caught by your grandma?" TJ teased. "Your *grandma,*" he said, emphasizing grandma to rub it in even more.

"Fine. Okay, let's go," I said. "This better be fun." I slipped into a pair of denim shorts and a pink blouse. TJ stared at me impatiently, so I put on the first pair of shoes I found, my pink sandals. We walked outside. It was so dark in the forest that I couldn't see a thing. I held on to TJ's shirt and followed his lead.

"Where are we going?" Curiosity was getting the best of me.

"Can you be patient? I have to hurry … before sunrise." TJ picked up the pace. I grew a little irritated because I was kind of being dragged. Somehow, we made it to a plain. The entire plain was barren, with the exception of a single tree. He told me to look up. The stars shone brightly and lustrously in the night sky. They seemed to form the outline of a lady.

"That's one of the angels," TJ said, pointing her out. He lay on the grass and stared into the sky. "It's prettier seeing the stars from earth than being in the sky with them."

I lay on the grass next to him and stared at the sky, too. I enjoyed the nice, cool, morning breeze.

"What time does granny wake up?" TJ said.

"Beats me. I haven't stayed with her in years," I said, yawning. Apparently, being dragged through the woods had not done much to awaken me. The sun slowly climbed up the horizon. "Well, we should go back." I rose from the grass.

"You're so boring," TJ said, sighing and dragging after me.

"Really, I'm boring? You're the one who woke me up all early just to look at stars!"

"But they were pretty. I wanted to show you other things besides your crazy party life." His response angered me, but I was left speechless. We walked back to my grandmother's cabin in silence. I slowly creaked open the door; the lights were still off. Good, Grandma was still asleep. I tiptoed to my room, climbed into bed, and wrapped my body in the sheets. Footsteps wandered close to my room. *Grandma!* I pretended to be asleep. My grandmother tapped me to awaken me.

"Come on to town with me today," Grandma said. "We are having a community get-together."

TJ mouthed "Boring." I ignored him and turned away.

"Yeah, I will come with you today," I responded. TJ sighed. Grandma happily walked out my room, and I closed my door to pretend to get dressed.

"Why did you agree to go? You know old people are boring," whined TJ.

"Well, you know what TJ? You don't have to come. Better yet, you don't have to be my angel, because you're being immature!" I snapped and stormed out of the room. I ignored him and got into the car with Grandma. I turned on my iPod and stared out the window. Grandma stared at me in the rearview mirror and turned her music up to drown out the music blaring from my headphones.

TJ appeared next to me. "Are you mad at me?" TJ asked.

Irritated, I looked at him.

"Um, yeah," I whispered fiercely. "You are being really annoying." TJ gasped in shock. Saddened, he reached for my hand.

"Look, Jalissa, I'm sorry. I really don't want you to be mad at me. I want to continue guarding and protecting you … and making you laugh," he said.

"Um, okay," I answered. Next thing I knew, I turned to see TJ balling right before me. Of course, he was putting on an act, but I could tell he said what he meant.

"Hey, hey, there's no need for that. I forgive you, okay?" I patted his shoulder gently. Slowly, TJ's hands slid from his face and revealed a huge smile. He threw his arms around me and squeezed tightly.

"I knew you would forgive me!" TJ exclaimed.

"I knew you were putting on an act, but you meant what you said when you repented," I said. TJ smirked.

"Okay, let's not get ahead of yourself, Ms. Smarty-pants. I am *the* master of acting," said TJ.

"Sure you are." Sarcasm dripped from my response. "I know this is kind of random, but how old are you?"

"That's a good question. I don't know; angels don't really have an age," answered TJ. "I guess I am as old as you."

"Hmm, well, okay, do you wish you could be human?"

"You sure are asking a lot of questions," he said. "Sometimes I wish I could be seen. I don't like people thinking you're deranged or crazy just because you talk to me."

"Aw, how considerate of you," I said. TJ smiled and batted his eyes like a bashful schoolgirl.

"You're welcome," he said, still pretending to be bashful. I giggled at his little impression.

"So how long is it to town?" TJ asked and did air quotes with his fingers around the word town.

"It's not that long. From what I remember, it's going to be about twenty minutes," I answered.

"Okey dokey. Wake me up when we get there," sighed TJ and laid his head on my shoulder. In a matter of seconds, he was fast asleep. I stared at him for a little while and smiled. Humph, he fell asleep on the job. With no one to talk to, I let my mind drift away into the music.

*   *   *

The car came to a halt. I slowly opened my eyes; I hadn't realized I was sleeping. TJ made himself comfortable on my right side. He was still asleep. Guarding me must have drained him. I gently tapped his shoulder to awaken him. Moving like molasses, he took his time waking up and stretching. I guess he thought he had all the time in the world. I peered out of the window. We were in town at the park. Kids ran and played jubilantly while adults gossiped and laughed. The smell of barbeque seized my attention. Ah, there it is. A man grilled steak, hamburgers, and hot dogs.

"Check it out! Food!" exclaimed TJ as he energetically exited the car. Apparently, the tantalizing aroma caught his attention, too. Grandma unloaded paper plates from her car. She called me over to help her take the paper cups to the table. I scooped up the cups and followed.

"Just place those cups on the table. Wait right here," said Grandma. "There is somebody I would like you to meet." A pale-skinned lady with short brown hair approached with a similarly pale-skinned, long-brown-haired teenager in tow.

"This is Mrs. Shelia and her granddaughter, Penela," Grandma said, introducing me to the ladies. "This is my granddaughter, Jalissa." I shook both of their hands.

"It's nice to meet you, Jalissa," said Penela.

"Nice to meet you, too." I responded politely. TJ stared off into the distance. He was in his own little world.

"Well," said Grandma as she turned to walk away, "we are going to help out over there while you two get acquainted." Penela happily waved good-bye to Mrs. Shelia. Her happiness was feigned. As soon as her grandmother looked away, Penela turned and frowned at me.

"Geez, what's her problem?" TJ asked.

Without thinking, I responded aloud, "I don't know."

"Hey, did you say something?" Penela asked.

"Me? Oh, no. Not me." My response was hesitant. I hoped she didn't think I was crazy.

"Oh, well I hate when my grandma does this to me," Penela rambled in a frustrated tone. "I'm sixteen years old, and she's trying to arrange little play dates for me, no offense to you."

"Um, none taken. I understand."

"I'm a big girl now. I know how to make friends. Besides, this town is boring," griped Penela.

"She's not lying," added TJ. He kicked a rock to punctuate his comment.

"There are no parties, no cute boys," groused Penela, "just a bunch of boring people."

"Oh, I'm cute. Don't you agree?" TJ asked excitedly.

"Yeah. It doesn't really matter though; She can't see you." I retorted.

"So you *do* think I'm cute." TJ gave me a playful nudge.

"What?" I cried out. "I was just answering your question!" I tried to explain. I didn't realize I said it aloud … *again*.

"Um, answer what question?" Penela asked.

"Uh, um, about the play date thing, remember?" I tried to make sense. TJ looked at me and smiled. He enjoyed watching me suffer embarrassment a little too much for my taste.

"Oh, okay. You're a little strange, but you're nice. We should hang out more," suggested Penela.

"Oh, yeah sure. That'd be great." We exchanged numbers.

* * *

"Let's get going home. It's getting late," said Grandma. I said my good-byes to Penela, and Grandma and I headed back home. We finally made it back home. Grandma told me she was heading to bed early because in the morning, she had to run some errands in town. I went to my room and lay on my bed. TJ followed. He lay on the floor and stared at the ceiling.

Out of the corner of my eye, I saw something glowing. I looked out of the window and saw a glowing, white ball hovering outside my window.

"Hey! TJ look! What's that?" I said, pointing. Startled, he jumped up and looked out the window.

It wasn't there anymore.

"Hey, there's nothing there. You trying to pull a prank on me?" TJ peered at me suspiciously.

"No really. It was there!"

"Whoa. Wait a minute," responded TJ with a look of realization on his face. "You saw a spirit?" TJ looked astonished. It seemed like he was telling me more than asking me.

"Well, I guess. If that's what it was." TJ's assertion further piqued my curiosity about … um, whatever it was. "Hey, let's go outside and look," I said. TJ agreed, so we went outside to search for it. I looked toward the lake and saw the white ball floating in that direction. TJ gasped.

"Hey, I see it now. Let's follow it." TJ walked in the direction of the glow. Together, we discreetly stalked the spirit. It came to a halt when it neared the shoreline. We stopped and hid behind a tree to await the orb's next move. I glanced over at TJ as the ball evolved into a transparent female entity. She looked about the age of a young adult, and she had long white hair. She also appeared very sad. She glanced about skeptically. TJ and I continued to hide behind the tree. We didn't want to alert the wayfaring soul to our presence.

I moved in to get a closer look. She had long, framed bangs that covered her brows and sphere-shaped eyes. Not noticing we were there, she faced forward and proceeded to the shore of the lake. She took graceful steps into the water. She ventured further into the water until her entire body was submerged. Suddenly, the entire lake bubbled like it was boiling. TJ and I watched in amazement from behind the tree. A floating city rose from the bubbles. Lights from the buildings flashed on all at once. I rubbed my eyes to make sure I saw things clearly. The floating city was still there.

"What should we do?" I asked TJ.

"Let's go explore it!" TJ exclaimed. We approached the shore. A floating wooden path led from the shoreline to the threshold of the city. TJ instructed me to wait on the shore while he tested the bridge to see if it was safe enough to cross.

"It's safe, let's go." TJ grabbed my hand and helped me onto the bridge. Chills ran throughout my body. I sensed that, unlike TJ, these ghastly spirits were deceased people. He was different; I felt positive energy and warmth around him. Two colossal, knighted statues vigilantly guarded the entrance to the city. I wondered if they were spirits also. TJ looked at me and gulped.

"Hey, why are you gulping? Aren't you supposed to be the brave angel that protects me?" I said.

"I am that vigilant protector. I was just messing with you when I did that. Okay, wait here. I'll take care of this." TJ approached the colossal statues. I waited and watched him explain something to them. The statues looked at each other and nodded their heads simultaneously and moved aside. I was astonished. TJ turned and waved for me to come. He took my arm and led me past the guards. They watched as we entered the ancient city. All kinds of unique looking spirits roamed the city.

"Hey, what did you tell those knights anyway?" I asked. TJ chuckled a bit and grinned a sly grin.

"Well, I told them I was a messenger from the creator, and you were my, um, disciple," he explained.

"Disciple?" I repeated with raised eyebrows.

"Hey, c'mon. We're in, aren't we?" TJ added. I smiled a little bit.

"Yeah, I guess," I answered as I scoped around.

"Hey, look, there's that girl." TJ pointed at the girl as she entered an elaborate palace. We pursued the eerie girl. I wondered if she was leading us on purpose. We slowly creaked open the palace doors and revealed an empty ballroom with stained glass windows of celestial figures.

"Hey, that kind of looks like me on that window!" TJ pointed at the design on one of the windows. I examined the window. It *did* look a lot like him. The character in the window looked like he was jumping up in the air. "What an interesting coincidence," I thought. "It looks energetic like him, too." My fascination with the stained glass window was interrupted when I saw the girl climb up a marble staircase and head into a corridor. TJ and I looked at each other. As if we read each other's minds, we paced after her up the steps. We stopped at the corner of the intersection of the corridor and waited.

"Okay, wait here while I make sure the coast

is clear." Like a goofy spy, TJ tucked and rolled to the other corner.

"Um, what are you doing?" I asked him with a smirk.

"Shhh! I'm a spy," TJ hushed me. "Dun dun nuh nuh nuh dun nuh dun nuh nuh." He sang the international spy song and did a cartwheel back to where I stood. I laughed at his silliness.

"Okay, Mr. Spy, you done?" I asked.

"Uh huh, let's go!" TJ peeked into the hallway just as the girl entered another door.

"Geez, she sure is evasive," TJ said. We hurried and crept through the corridor after the girl. She stopped at the spire of the palace. TJ stood in front of me as she slowly turned around.

"You can see us," the girl spoke softly and pointed at me.

"Who? Me?" TJ pointed at himself.

"No, the human girl," said the mysterious girl. TJ frowned then stood aside.

"You have to help us. Our souls cannot move on from this world."

"She's got a name, you know." TJ folded his arms.

"My apologies, Jalissa. I am Nylana, spirit of the lake."

"How do you know my name, and what do you want me to do?" I asked.

"Long ago, a witch cursed our palace because she

envied our kingdom. She punished us by trapping our souls in crystals and scattering them about. There are ten of them hidden in various places. You must find them and bring them to us," Nylana said and then vanished.

Suddenly, there was a flash of light; TJ and I ended up back on the shore.

"What am I supposed to do, TJ?" I was worried by Nylana's request.

"I think we should help them," he responded. I sighed. That seemed like an enormous task to take on.

We walked back to the cabin in silence. I put on my pajamas and laid on my bed in darkness. TJ lay on my floor. I wasn't sure if he was asleep or not.

"Hey, TJ. She never answered my question about how she knew my name. This is kind of creepy," I said. TJ didn't respond. I scooted to the corner of my bed and saw that he had his hands behind his head and was staring at the ceiling.

"Hey, did you hear me?"

"Yeah, sorry. I was just thinking." TJ gave me his attention.

"Oh, about what?"

"It's nothing. You better get some sleep, though."

"Okay. Well, goodnight." I scooted back into the center of the bed. I couldn't shake the feeling that something was bothering him, or he was hiding something.

Either way, it kind of bothered me that he didn't want to share how he felt.

Chapter 3

Crystal Retrieval

As I stood in the forest, I heard disquieting tunes that shook my spirit. I was paranoid and clueless. I looked around everywhere for TJ. I was alone. The transparent floating orb appeared. I sensed that it wanted me to follow it, so I acquiesced. The trail was familiar; this was the same forest that surrounded my grandmother's cabin. The orb entered a pitch-black cave. Hesitantly, I entered the cave. Suddenly, there was a burst of white light, and a voice chimed in my head, saying, "It is here. Retrieve it."

I awakened in my room. TJ rested peacefully on the floor. I looked out the window to see it was barely morning. "Hmm," I thought. "I guess Nylana led me to the first crystal." I slid off my bed and sat next to him. I tapped on his shoulder until he awakened. Slowly, he stretched and got up.

"I know where one of the crystals is located."

"How do you know?" TJ asked.

"I had a vision in my dream. Nylana showed me where it was."

"Alrighty then, let's get going," TJ said. We left my grandma's cabin in search of the crystal. The clouds were dark and ominous; it looked like it was about to rain. The trail I dreamed about was committed to memory, so navigation was effortless. I carefully observed the landmarks to ensure they matched the ones from my dream. A cool breeze blew from the north.

"That must be where the crystal is," TJ inferred. We walked in the direction of the guiding wind and finally approached the cave Nylana revealed in my dream. It was darker and more mysterious in reality. We entered. I couldn't see a thing, but apparently TJ could. I held onto his shirt as we walked deeper and deeper into the cave. As we walked, I tripped over something. I screeched and fell flat on my face. TJ stopped when he noticed I wasn't holding onto his shirt. He turned and helped me up from the ground.

"Ha, you okay?" TJ asked, chuckling a bit.

"Yeah, I'm fine." I brushed my clothes off. I turned around and saw a glowing red light.

"Hey, TJ. I think I found it." I picked up the glowing red object. It was a crystal. "Let's go back to the lake and give it to Nylana."

We headed for the cave opening, but I stopped at the entrance because it was raining heavily.

"Oh, crap." I made no effort to advance into the downpour.

"What's the matter? It's just rain," TJ said.

"Just rain? Whatever. I don't want to get my hair wet. It'll get all frizzy."

"Fine. Well, let's just sit here for a while then." TJ sat on a ledge near the entrance. I dusted off my clothes and sat next to him. TJ stared at the rain. He was contemplating something. I examined the crystal in my hand. It was small, and I could feel vibrations as energy radiated from within. The crystal shimmered in my hand as I held it up to the sky for further examination. I turned to see TJ still looking off into the distance.

I poked him. "Hey, what are you thinking about?" He quickly snapped out his trance.

"I can't feel the rain," he said softly, almost ashamed.

"Hey, it's not all that. I mean, *it's just rain,*" I said in an attempt to cheer him up. TJ always joked around, but he actually seemed serious this time. I placed my hand on his shoulder to comfort him.

"We just need to hurry and help the spirits with these crystals," TJ said in a monotone. I smiled at him.

"Aw, TJ likes the rain," I quipped in a squeaky voice. I reached over and pinched his cheeks playfully.

"Agh! Hey, cut it out!" He laughed and brushed my hand away.

"Come on!" I stood up and pulled TJ from the ground

and into the rain with me. My hair and clothes were soaked in no time. TJ's spiked hair drooped down over his face. At this point, I decided not to be concerned about my hair getting wet. I wanted to cheer him up.

"So you couldn't feel the water in the lake either?" I said.

"Nope. It just feels like empty space."

"But you … were swimming," I said.

He looked up at the sky. A slight frown came across my face, but then I smiled.

"You're all wet, though," I said.

"Yeah, I know," answered TJ.

"But you can feel me right?" I said.

"Yeah, you're the only person I can feel," he said. I started spinning in the rain. I got dizzy so I stopped and looked down at my feet. My shoes were all muddy.

"Eww, Jalissa has brown feet," TJ teased.

"Whatever, I got pretty brown feet," I said and kicked my feet in the mud. In the midst of the tomfoolery, my mind drifted back to the reason we were here. "You think that floating city is there right now?"

"Why don't we go check it out?" TJ suggested. I agreed. We walked in the rain to the lake. As we approached the shore, we realized the floating city was nowhere in sight.

"Great, it's not even here," TJ said.

"Maybe we can summon it somehow," I said. I

looked around. I pulled out the crystal from the cave and held it up to the sky. I stared hopefully at the lake, wondering if the city would surface. *Nothing.* It didn't work. Disappointed, I put down the crystal.

"I guess it didn't work. Let's try later," suggested TJ. We headed home until we heard a familiar bubbling sound. We faced the lake and saw the imaginary city had surfaced.

"Hey, good job. I guess it worked," said TJ. We ran to the bridge. The knightly statues that guarded the entrance had already moved aside. "Maybe they were expecting us," I thought. TJ stopped before he passed the guards and waited for me.

"Let's stick together, okay?" He held my arm and walked me past the guards. We passed the guards and saw Nylana a little further ahead. She looked as if she had been waiting for us.

"Well done, Jalissa, the creator has chosen this arrangement well," proclaimed Nylana.

"Huh?" I asked. I looked at TJ; he seemed kind of nervous.

"You will understand everything soon; everything will make sense in time," stated Nylana. I handed her the crystal. "There are nine more crystals you need to find. Once you retrieve all the crystals and bring them to us, we will be able to move on to the afterlife." She began approaching me with her graceful steps. It was kind of creepy. She stood before me and gazed right through my eyes. TJ watched in wonderment.

"I will show you where the next location is tonight," Nylana said, then disappeared. Chills rushed through my body. I closed my eyes and trembled. TJ and I left the floating city and headed back to my grandmother's cabin. I remembered the nervous expression on TJ's face when I questioned Nylana.

"Why did you look so nervous when Nylana was speaking to me back there? You're supposed to be my fearless guardian, remember?" I asked playfully and smiled.

"It's nothing. She kind of creeps me out," said TJ in a dry monotone. He looked at the ground, obviously pondering something.

"What is he hiding from me?" I wondered. "His actions are withdrawn. It's starting to worry me. I'll deal with it at an appropriate time."

We finally made it back to my grandmother's cabin. I looked around and saw the lights were off. Grandma must be out and about. I walked to the fridge and noticed a note posted on it: "Went to town to help decorate—love Grandma." I peeled the note from the fridge and yawned. I walked to my room and sat on my bed. I stretched and rubbed my eyes.

"You get tired easily," mentioned TJ.

"Yeah, these spirits got me running around

everywhere." I stretched out. As soon as I slipped on my pajamas, I closed my eyes and fell asleep.

Chapter 4

Forest Wayfarers

A stream flowed peacefully through a gorge. A rope and plank bridge dangled precariously over the stream. The floating, transparent orb levitated gracefully over the bridge. It was Nylana. She stopped near the end of the bridge and hovered like she was trying to attract my attention to something. There it was. A crystal stuck out from the side of the cliff near the end of the bridge.

I slowly awakened from my slumber. It was still dark outside. I glanced around my room and realized TJ wasn't there. "He's always here," I thought. "Where is he now?"

I panicked and whispered his name desperately, hoping I didn't wake up Grandma. I sneaked outside. The full moon illuminated the night sky and caused elongated shadows to fall from the trees. One shadow stood out from the rest. I followed the shadow and saw TJ sitting by a tree in the meadow. I approached him quietly. He sat in silence, gazing at the sky.

"Hey, I can see you from here," called TJ. "What brings you out here? Aren't you supposed to be sleeping?"

"Aren't you supposed to be watching me?" I shot back in response. I walked over to him and playfully ruffled his spiked hair. He fixed his hair back neatly. I sat next to him on the grass and took a deep breath. Together, we gazed at the sky.

"I had another vision," I said. "Nylana revealed the location of the next crystal."

"We need to hurry and collect these crystals and return them to Nylana."

"What's up with you? Is something bugging you?" His tone worried me. TJ was a constant clown. This serious TJ was disconcerting. The moon began to set as the sun slowly ascended into the sky.

"No, it's nothing. So where's the next crystal?" TJ hopped up and stretched. I temporarily ignored how he changed the subject, but I promised myself I'd find out what he was hiding sooner or later.

"It is near a gorge that has a rope and plank bridge suspended over a stream." I stood up and walked in the direction of where I thought the next crystal was located. TJ trotted after me. We finally made it to a bridge similar to the one in my vision. The crystal was mounted on the cliff side.

"How are we supposed to get that?" TJ surveyed the

area for a solution. I looked too. I spotted a rope lying on the ground near the bridge.

"Over there!" I pointed at the rope. I ran toward it, picked it up, and wrapped it around my slim waist. I tied the other end firmly around a nearby tree. TJ watched me in awe. I tugged at the rope with all my might to test its sturdiness. The knot didn't budge.

"Alright, I'm going down." I repelled down the side of the cliff. TJ paced back and forth and watched me like a hawk. I finally reached the crystal. I gripped it tightly and pulled as hard as I could. Then I tried wiggling the crystal around. It worked. The golden crystal loosened enough to be pried from the cliff side. I pulled myself up, untied the rope from my waist, and dusted myself off.

"Go, Jalissa! It's your birthday!" sang TJ as he applauded and cheered. I giggled.

"Okay, cheerleader," I said, embarrassed. "Let's take this back to Nylana."

* * *

As we approached the lake, I proudly held the crystal up to the sky and announced my triumphant retrieval. The lake bubbled, and the floating city began to rise. TJ and I walked across the bridge. The vigilant guards parted to reveal Nylana waiting patiently behind them. She held out both of her hands as we approached. I handed over the crystal. She looked first at TJ and then at me. She nodded her head once in approval and disappeared. TJ and I exited the bridge and were on our way back to my grandmother's cabin.

The cabin was empty. My grandmother was out and about again. Exhausted and drained from all the running around to acquire the crystal, I fell back on my bed like a rag doll.

The transparent orb maneuvered down a path until it reached a misty bog. The fog was extremely dense. The orb moved further west and halted near three marble angel fountains. The two side fountains spouted steady streams of water. I assumed the crystal was clogging the middle fountain's flow. I examined the fountain further; my assumptions were correct. A lavender colored crystal clogged the fountain's opening. It was an amethyst.

I abruptly arose from my slumber. I hadn't realized I had dozed off. I got up from my bed and found TJ wandering around in the kitchen.

"I assume you know where the next crystal is," said TJ. I yawned and stretched.

"Yeah, we better get going." I slipped on some shoes and a bright blue t-shirt and some tan shorts.

"So where are we headed, captain?" asked TJ.

"To a misty bog," I responded, "There are angel fountains there. One of them is being clogged by the crystal." We ventured into the depths of the forest.

Strange whispers and animal sounds echoed all around us. The mist grew thicker.

"This is creepy." I grabbed TJ's arm. He pulled me closer to make sure we didn't get separated. The mist condensed as we approached the enormous marble angel fountains. There they were—the two functional fountains flanking the congested fountain. The center, clogged angel fountain held a trumpet. The glow of the amethyst radiated from inside the bell of the trumpet. It was out of my reach. *If only if I was a little taller*.

"Hey, I can lift you up so you can get the crystal," suggested TJ. I gasped in amazement. *Did he read my mind?*

"Good idea. Let's do this," I said. TJ squatted and reached his arms out for me to step up. I obliged, and he lifted me high enough to reach inside the bell of the trumpet. I reached inside and felt around. I managed to firmly grasp the crystal and tug at it. Finally, the crystal wrenched free from the trumpet. I examined the crystal. It was beautiful.

A weird sound came from inside the bell of the trumpet. I took a peek. *Whoosh!* The water rushed out ferociously. The impact knocked me off my feet, and I fell backward. Fortunately, TJ caught me just before I hit the base of the fountain. My face and hair were soaked.

"Look on the bright side, at least the fountain is working again," TJ said.

"At least I got the crystal," I said, sighing as I stashed the amethyst in my pocket. I wiped my eyes. TJ set me down gently.

"True," TJ said, nodding. "Let's return this crystal to Nylana." We walked toward the lake. As we neared the shoreline, we saw that the floating city had already arisen from the watery depths. "Hmm," I thought. "Nylana must be expecting us." TJ and I crossed the bridge and found Nylana waiting at the city's gateway.

"Well done. The two of you are on a roll. This is a great deal for us both." Nylana spoke to me, but she gazed at TJ.

"All right, we'll just keep getting your crystals, so you can crossover," said TJ. He grabbed my arm and dragged me off the bridge. I wrested my arm away from his grip and stood facing with him.

"What the heck is the matter with you, huh?" I asked. TJ looked away briefly but turned back and stared into my eyes.

"It's nothing," he said. "Let's just get these crystals to Nylana." He brushed me off and stepped around me.

"Don't you walk away while I'm talking to you! There's something up between you and Nylana, isn't there?" I said.

"What? No! I don't know. She was just looking at

me." He sounded unsure of his response. "Oh, you're jealous I see." TJ grinned.

"Huh, uh, no! Of course not!" I said.

"Don't worry. I totally understand if you are, because I ain't no ugly duckling, sister girl!" TJ said with pride.

"Oh my gosh, you are so conceited." I turned my back to him and started walking home. He shrugged and walked after me.

* * *

I entered my room and closed the door. I wiped my face with my hands. Recovering crystals had made me weary. I reminisced on how I ended up having an angel and communicating with spirits. I realized I never questioned this venture; I just kind of went along with everything. It was strange how these supernatural occurrences didn't seem to bother me. I wondered if these things would frighten the average teenager. Which brought up another question: Why did TJ come here in the first place? Why did he come at this particular time in my life? Anyway, I remained optimistic. Everything is connected, and I was sure these ties would soon weave together.

"I'm going to get some sleep so I can find the location of the next crystal."

"Alright then, nighty night," concluded TJ.

*　*　*

The transparent orb moved steadily down the path until it reached an ancient tree. The roots of the aged tree extended deep into the earth's soil. The tree appeared to be twenty feet wide and seventy feet high. There was an unusually large hole in the tree about thirty feet up. A peridot crystal lay inside the hole.

I sprang from my sleep.

Chapter 5

Tree of Antiquity

I awakened to the sound of giggling. TJ was laughing at me because I woke up startled. I wiped my droopy eyes and grinned.

"Hey, you okay?" TJ asked, still giggling.

"I'm fine. I figured out where the next crystal is hidden." I put clothes on over my pajamas. There really was no point in changing my wardrobe, because when I came back, I'd be going to sleep again to receive the location of the next crystal. TJ and I were headed to the door when my grandmother spotted me.

"Where you going, girlie?" asked Grandma. I froze and looked at TJ desperately.

"Tell her you're taking a morning stroll to get some fresh air," advised TJ. I nodded.

"Um, I'm taking a morning stroll to get some fresh air," I repeated softly.

"Oh! I'm so glad you're enjoying it out this way. You

have fun, dear," concluded Grandma. She sauntered to her room. TJ and I continued outside.

"Phew, that was a close one," I said, sighing in relief.

"Hey, it was a close one thanks to me!" TJ said proudly.

"Yeah, you're right, buddy," I smiled, "Thanks TJ." I patted him on the back. "Anyway, I—"

"Jalissa, I need to tell you something," interrupted TJ. I looked at him apprehensively. Maybe he was finally going to tell me what was bothering him.

"Wha … what is it?" I asked. TJ stared at me silently. He turned away.

"It's nothing," dismissed TJ and walked on. I jogged to catch up with him; I was anxious to hear what he had to say. It was interesting to listen to what he had to say. He was a mysterious person, or being.

"C'mon, you can tell me. We've been friends for a while," I said.

"You actually called me your friend!" TJ said. I gave him a puzzled look.

"Yeah, I did," I acknowledged. "You are my angel … and friend."

"I just wanted to tell you that your hair looks pretty," said TJ, smiling.

"Thanks, but I'm pretty sure you wanted to tell me something on a more serious note."

"Oh, c'mon, take the compliment. You don't have to

be all analytical," said TJ. "Anyway, what's it going to take to get the next crystal?"

"Um, I don't know, but I have to climb a tree to get it."

"Nothing like some fun tree climbing," added TJ.

"Well, it's supposed to be in a hole in a large, old tree," I said as we approached the old tree.

"Whoa! This tree is huge," gasped TJ with his mouth wide open. I looked upward and examined the tree to see if I could spot the hole that contained the peridot crystal. I finally found the hole and saw a shiny, lime green glow emanating from inside. I assumed it was the crystal.

"All right, I'm climbing up." I tightened my sneakers.

"Be careful. Don't worry, if you fall, I'll be right here to catch you." TJ watched me cautiously make my first steps up the tree. I slowly ascended the tree. I felt strange energy vibrations radiating from the tree. They must have come from the crystal. I finally reached the colossal hole. It was so big my whole body fit inside. I sat inside and rested. I retrieved the crystal and showed it to TJ.

"I've got it!" I exclaimed excitedly while I waved the crystal around. TJ smiled. He had this weird sparkly look in his eyes, and I think I did, too. TJ flew up to the tree to get me so I wouldn't have to climb down.

"Why didn't you fly me up to the hole instead of letting me do all that work?" I said.

TJ chuckled and scratched his head. "Sorry, I didn't realize I could do that, and I thought you could use a little exercise."

"You made me climb that tree for nothing." I frowned and pushed him aside.

"Hey, c'mon. I wouldn't let anything happen to you," said TJ.

* * *

"TJ, this is random, but I have to ask."

"What's eatin' ya, Lissa?" He sat on the ground.

"Well—"

"Jalissa!" My explanation was interrupted by a vaguely familiar voice. I looked up and saw Penela running toward me.

"Great, and I was anxious to hear what you had to say," TJ complained. He frowned and stood up.

"Hey, what are you doing out in the woods all by your lonesome?" said Penela.

"Huh? Who talks like that? Plus, you're not by yourself. You're with one of the best angels ever created," said TJ.

"You can't be heard," I said out loud.

"You can't hear me?" Penela asked. She looked puzzled.

"Um, uh, yeah, I can hear you ... now. Sorry, I have a lot on my mind," I answered.

"You're really weird, you always seem distracted," said Penela. "Maybe it's the wilderness that's got you buggin'. Anyway, I'll see you later. I got to fetch some wood for my grandma." She walked off into the distance.

"Now that she is gone, what did you want to ask me?" TJ said, giving me his undivided attention.

"Why do you like earth so much? I mean, it's so imperfect here, and I can't stand the way people treat each other sometimes," I said.

"Go on."

"I don't see why people hurt each other," I said. "We are all going to die sooner or later, so why can't we help each other out while we're here? I wished we lived in an age of no more tears and pain." TJ stared at me in awe and smiled.

"You don't happen to have any sharp objects?" asked TJ.

"Uh, no," I said.

"Do you have any materials that may cause a short-age of breath?" TJ asked with suspicious, playful eyes.

"What! No! I'm not suicidal." I nudged him.

"I know you aren't. I was just kidding with you," said TJ. "But sometimes, being an angel and all that, you get tired of perfection."

I smiled and soaked in his sense of humor like a sponge.

"Let's get this crystal to Nylana," he said. We headed back to the lake.

* * *

Again, the floating city was already surfaced. Nylana stood on the bridge near the city's entrance. TJ and I crossed the bridge arm in arm. I handed the peridot crystal over to Nylana. She thanked us, nodded her head once, and disappeared into thin air.

"Only six more crystals," I said as we walked back to my grandmother's house.

"Yeah, you better get some sleep, so the location of the next crystal can be revealed."

* * *

We entered the cabin. I went to my room and reflected on how the days seemed to pass so quickly. I wondered what would happen after I retrieved all the crystals. Would the floating city disappear? Would TJ disappear with them, because he was considered a spirit? These questions rang in my thoughts. I was starting to enjoy his company.

The plush forest opened to expose a hidden clearing. Climbing vines concealed a tall, black gate. A huge abandoned brick mansion peeked through the bars of the gate. There was a stunning white flash. I awakened knowing the whereabouts of the next crystal.

Chapter 6

Wayward Soul

Iglanced around the room, looking for TJ. He was nowhere in sight. I got up from bed to look for him. I found him in the living room listening to my iPod. His back was to me, so he was unaware that I was watching from my bedroom as he danced and lip-synced to the music. He held a brush and pretended it was a microphone. He looked so silly that I had to chuckle. When he turned around to finish up one of his dance routines, he noticed me. He froze like a statue. He was awkwardly silent for a few seconds, and then he laughed. Mildly embarrassed, he turned the iPod off and handed it to me.

"Sorry, I got a little bored while you were sleeping." He looked downward and rubbed his head.

"It's okay, I would've been bored, too." I tried to ease his embarrassment, but I was still laughing at him.

"So do you know where the next crystal is?" TJ asked.

"Yeah, I think it's in an abandoned mansion in the

forest. My dream didn't pinpoint exactly where it is in the mansion, so we'll have to search it."

* * *

We left my grandmother's cabin and walked to the clearing in the forest. Once we stepped into the clearing, the black gate covered in clinging vines greeted us. The melancholy mansion rested behind it. It looked exactly as it did in my dream. TJ walked up to the gate and tugged at it.

"It's locked." A look of disgust spread across his face. "What do we do now?"

"Well, maybe you can use that little flying technique you used to help me out of that big tree," I suggested.

"Oh yeah, I didn't think of that."

"Of course not. Why would you? You're just the angel," I said.

"Okay, Miss Smarty-pants, just get on my back so I can get you to the other side," said TJ. I climbed onto his back.

"Whoa, you're heavy!" He pretended to wobble like he was going to drop me.

"Hey, I'm not fat!"

"Calm down, I was just kidding with ya. You're as light as a feather."

I looked into the sky as we slowly maneuvered up

into the air. TJ set us down on the other side of the gate. The grass was up to my knees.

"Geez, this grass needs a haircut," TJ joked as we approached the mansion's colossal doors. "What's a mansion doing in the middle of a forest anyway?"

"I don't know."

I pushed open the mansion's doors. Inside it was dim and dusty. Rays of sunlight pierced the room through small holes in the windows. We explored the room. Furniture covered in white sheets littered the room. Suddenly, I heard the sound of a child laughing and playing. TJ rushed to my side.

"Where's that coming from?" I asked. I grabbed him. He remained close to me and scanned the room. A striped red and green ball rolled into the foyer from another room. I nervously looked at TJ.

"Maybe the crystal is in there," I suggested.

"Jalissa, this is a spirit. Let me walk in there first," said TJ. "Stay close to me." I held onto him tightly as he guided me toward the room from where the ball appeared. We crossed the threshold of the room. There was a newspaper lying in the center of the floor. Figuring it was a clue, I picked up the newspaper and saw it was dated four years earlier. The headline read "Missing Boy." A picture of a pale-faced boy with dirty blond, curly hair illustrated the headline. He held a ball in his hand identical to the one that had rolled into the foyer. I read on. The boy had green eyes. His name was Heido. TJ and I exchanged flabbergasted glances.

"TJ, I think Heido is the spirit in this mansion. Poor Heido." We walked back into the foyer. On my peripheral, I saw a figure standing atop the staircase. Heido stood there with a bright blue, aquamarine crystal. He had a forlorn expression.

"TJ, look, he has the crystal." I pointed at Heido. TJ flew up to where Heido was.

"Heido, I'm so sorry about what happened to you," said TJ. "We really need that crystal to help the spirits of the lake cross over." Heido remained silent. He turned his gaze toward me. His expression totally freaked me out. A newspaper flew into the air and landed at my feet. I looked back at him, and then picked up the paper. There was a picture of Penela, Mrs. Shelia, and Heido standing together. Penela appeared to be his older sister. I covered my mouth with my hand.

"Penela wanders these woods in hopes of finding me," Heido finally spoke. "She will be here, outside the gates, in about five minutes. My soul is trapped inside this mansion. Give this to her." He tossed a silver bracelet to me. "In exchange, I will give you the crystal."

TJ flew downstairs, and we walked outside to await Penela's arrival.

"Hurry," I demanded. "Take me to the other side of the gate." TJ swept me off my feet and whisked me to the other side of the gate. I heard someone coming, so I pretended to look around.

"Jalissa, what are you doing here?" Penela asked.

"Well, I was just taking a nature stroll," I said, fishing for an explanation. "I got sidetracked by this mansion. I've never seen one in a forest before. Look, I found this bracelet on my stroll." I handed the bracelet to Penela. She examined it. She looked up at me quickly and back down at the bracelet. Then she fell to her knees.

"Heido?" Penela murmured with tears streaming down her cheeks. I embraced her.

"Heido is my brother," she said, wiping away tears. "He's been missing for four years now. I'm so glad you found this. I really have to go now, though. I'm supposed to be getting wood for my grandma again. Thank you." Penela slipped on the bracelet and scurried away.

* * *

TJ and I entered the mansion and saw Heido standing in the foyer. His forlorn expression had vanished—now he looked content as he happily approached us.

"Thank you, Jalissa and TJ. There's a very bright future for the both of you," Heido announced as he handed me the aquamarine crystal. A glowing white light appeared behind him. He walked into it. Heido had crossed over.

* * *

"I'm glad Heido was able to cross over," I said to TJ as we headed to the lake.

"Me, too. Now his soul can forever rest in peace. You know, when people are alive, they fear death," said TJ. "Then the people who mourn death are sometimes suffering in life while the deceased are resting in peace."

"Yeah, that's true," I agreed.

We were close enough to see the lake. The floating city had already surfaced. Nylana stood at the threshold of the city on the bridge.

"It was quite a mission to retrieve this crystal," stated Nylana as I handed her the crystal. "Good job you two." She vanished.

TJ and I exited the bridge and headed back to my grandmother's cabin.

"Hey, will you cross over, and if you do, when?" I asked. "Don't get offended or anything. It's not like I don't like having you around." TJ stopped walking and frowned a little. Maybe I offended him. I felt bad for asking. "I'm sorry if I upset you or anything by asking you that question."

"No, I'm not mad," replied TJ. "I'm just a little surprised you're concerned."

"What, I can't wonder?" I asked with a little smile.

"Sure you can!" he exclaimed. "To be honest, I really don't know." TJ put his hands behind his head.

"Well, I think you're a really good friend, and I don't want you to go."

"Once again, I'm shocked," said TJ with a smile.

"Why are you shocked?" I asked.

"Well, when I first met you, you had an attitude with me all the time. I thought you didn't care much to have me around," he said.

"No, that's not true. You were a little annoying until I got to know you better," I said. "Can you promise me that we'll stick together, wherever life takes us?"

He smiled. "I promise," he said. He walked over and hugged me.

"Okay, let's go so we can find the next crystal tomorrow," I said.

We finally made it to my grandmother's cabin. My grandmother sat in the living room, watching TV.

"Hey kiddo, where've you been?" she asked.

"I just wanted to take another stroll—it's pretty in the woods," I said.

"Oh okay, I'm glad that you enjoy it out this way," said Grandma. I smiled at her, walked to my room, and shut the door.

"Nice," congratulated TJ. "You didn't hesitate this time. Good job. Give me some dap." He put his hand up for me to give him a hand shake. I obliged.

I walked over to the bedroom window and opened

the curtains. I peeked outside. The waning moon and stars shone luminously in the sky.

"The stars are really beautiful tonight," I said. TJ gazed into the night sky.

"Well, I better get some sleep," I yawned. "We have to search for the next crystal tomorrow."

"Okay, goodnight Jalissa."

I fell backward onto my bed. TJ tucked me in under my comforter. I closed my eyes and drifted slowly into slumber.

Chapter 7

The Revelation

I slowly approached dense woods. The tall, crowded trees gradually revealed hidden ruins. Maybe it was once a temple, but now it was destroyed. A treasure chest lay at the heart of the temple. A white flash encumbered my vision. My eyes slowly opened.

TJ slept on the floor, leaning against the wall with his head tilted down. I climbed out of bed and gently tapped him on the shoulder. He slowly awakened.

"I know where the crystal is," I announced. TJ slowly stretched himself out. "You sleep okay?" I asked.

"Yeah, I'm fine. What did you see?"

"I saw ruins deep in the forest. There was a treasure chest somewhere in the ruins," I said. "I guess the crystal is in there."

"All right, let's get going," said TJ. We went outside to explore the forest. The summer breeze felt nice blowing across my face.

"School is going to start pretty soon," I said.

"Really, when?" asked TJ.

"I believe I have about a week left until school starts."

"Well, let's hurry and find the remaining crystals before you have to go back to school." Suddenly, an excited look came over TJ's face. "Hey look! The ruins!" he pointed. Debris and ancient ruins were scattered everywhere. The ruined stone temple from my dream was just ahead of us. At its main approach, two identical treasure chests were positioned side by side.

"Hey, there are two chests. I thought you only saw one?" said TJ.

"I did only see one in my dream. This is strange."

I inspected the chests. I decided to open the one to my right first. Slowly, the chest creaked open. A black orb levitated from the chest. Startled, I stumbled backward. I reoriented myself just in time to see the shadow-like orb hurtling toward me at full speed. My eyes bulged and my jaw dropped. I felt distraught and helpless. The orb plowed into my chest; I fell back in anticipation of the impact, but there was none. It went straight through me. I clutched my chest, dumbfounded. I looked back and saw the black orb transforming into a human-like form. I was stunned. It was me—except it wasn't really me, but a shadowy duplicate of me.

"Crap!" TJ slapped his hand on his head. "It's a doppelganger spirit!"

"What's a doppelganger spirit?"

"It's like a clone or a look-a-like of a person."

The doppelganger spirit opened the chest on the left, revealing an orange crystal.

"That's the crystal!" TJ said, pointing. The doppelganger looked at us mischievously before running off with the crystal.

"Let's go get the other you!" TJ said, running after the crystal snatcher. I ran to the treasure chest that formerly held the spirit. Inside, I found a scroll written in another language. I called for TJ. Maybe he could translate it. My call for assistance ended TJ's pursuit of the spirit. He immediately rushed to my side. With squinted eyes, he examined the scroll.

"Ye who releases the doppelganger spirit releases turmoil on thine own self," he read aloud. "Ye who wishes to be rid of the doppelganger spirit must reveal reflection upon it." TJ looked frustrated. "Great, so now we have to find a way for the doppelganger to see itself."

I remembered something and dug into my back pocket. "Hey, I have this little mirror."

"Well that's convenient," said TJ.

"Hey, a girl has to check how she looks once in a while."

"More like every five minutes." He laughed at his own joke.

"Okay, we're wasting time," I said, getting a little defensive. "Let's get this doppelganger."

I ran in the direction of the other me. It maneuvered through the dense woods, skillfully dodging trees. I have to admit that I was a bit impressed by this shadowy version of myself. It looked back and saw TJ and me in hot pursuit. It hastened its pace. Suddenly, it stopped abruptly. Its escape was cut short when it came upon the steep, rocky walls of a gorge. We had it cornered. I held up my mirror. The doppelganger stared into the mirror. With a shrill shriek, it exploded into a cloud of ashes. The whistling wind dissipated the ash cloud, exposing an orange crystal. TJ walked over and collected the orange colored crystal.

TJ identified the crystal as a sunstone. He also noticed there was something written on it. "The transformer," it read. I grasped the crystal and held it to the sky. The sun illuminated the precious stone.

"Let's take this to Nylana." I put the sunstone in my pocket. TJ and I headed back to the lake.

"Just four more crystals to go. Do you think we can get them all before I have to leave for school?"

"Of course, sure we can." TJ sounded so optimistic. His hopefulness made me smile.

* * *

The floating city seemed to be raised every time we arrived here now. I wondered if other people could see it floating atop the lake. Nylana stood on the bridge.

"Well done. You two are quite a team," said Nylana.

"Alright, here's the sunstone. We have to go now." TJ handed Nylana the crystal and abruptly turned to exit the bridge.

"Wait," Nylana said. "I must give Jalissa her vision now." She stared deep into my eyes.

A gentle spring cascaded over a cliff to create a beautiful waterfall. Fireflies twinkled above the water like metallic glitter. Rose petals floated atop the water. It looked so majestic. A chill swam through my body.

I snapped back to consciousness. "What was that place?"

"The scenery *is* quite captivating. It is the Soul Spring. You will find the rose quartz crystal there; however, you must visit it at night. Go tonight, the two of you, and return the crystal to me." Nylana vanished.

"Why tonight?" I wondered.

"Tonight is supposed to be the night of the mystical moon, and the spring is supposed to bring souls together," said TJ. "It's only a myth, though."

"That's interesting."

"Nightfall is just around the corner. We should get going to the Soul Spring."

"Okay, let's go." We walked into the forest. The twilight lit our path.

* * *

As we got closer to the spring, fireflies flitted into the night.

"Aw, this is beautiful," I gasped in wonder. TJ looked around in awe. He tried to gently capture a firefly in his hands. I chuckled at his youth-like innocence.

I neared the edge of the spring. The water looked so inviting. I stepped in. Warmth engulfed my entire body. It felt so peaceful.

"This is exuberating." I was completely relaxed.

TJ watched me from the shore with an enormous smile.

"What you starin' at?" I asked. His smile grew larger, and he joined me in the water. He swam around me.

"Hey, I noticed you've been kind of serious at times," I said. "What's up with that?"

TJ stopped swimming and came face to face with me. "What do you mean?"

"I don't know. I just feel you're not ..." I said, then I stopped. I was reluctant to express my feelings. "I just feel like something's bugging you, and it frustrates me because I can't pinpoint it."

TJ sighed and was silent for a moment. I looked

down. I wondered if he was offended. I looked up to see him looking down.

"Who am I fooling? You're a smart girl," TJ said. "I can't hide from you forever. You're right. Something is wrong."

"Can you tell me?" I said. "I've been dying to know."

"When we find all the crystals, the spirits will be free, and I will become human," said TJ. "At least that's what the creator says."

I was flabbergasted. Why didn't he tell me earlier? I would've worked extra hard to help him.

"Why didn't you tell me?" I asked, confused. "You knew all along and didn't even mention it?"

"Jalissa, I really wanted to be here, and I didn't want you to bail out on me."

"Why would you ever think I would do that to you?" I was shocked.

"Because being here is important to me."

"Why?"

"Because, darn it," TJ said, glancing up to the sky. Then I heard him whisper, "Not yet?" He wasn't talking to me—it seemed like he was repeating something he'd heard. TJ walked closer to me, gently grabbed my face, and kissed me on the cheek. My eyes widened, and then I closed them gently. He hugged me tightly. He released me and gazed into my eyes. I stared at him in shock.

"I can't answer that question yet," TJ finally said.

"*He* wants me to wait for the right time to reveal it to you." I stared at him in silence and gulped.

"Who's *he*?" I asked softly.

"The creator, God." He grabbed my hand and held it. "I would tell you why if I could. I'm sorry I can't." He looked into my eyes and said, "I just want you to know that I want and need to be here."

I stared at him and nodded my head. All of this was overwhelming yet comforting at the same time.

"Don't leave me, okay?" I said. "We will find these crystals." I hugged him. I didn't notice the tear on my cheek until TJ wiped it away.

"I'm not going anywhere, I promise." He held me and stared into my eyes. A pinkish object floated atop the water. I waded over to examine it. It was a heart-shaped, rose-colored, quartz crystal.

"Nice timing," I said as I picked up the rose quartz. I examined it before putting it in my pocket.

"You ready to take it to Nylana?" asked TJ.

"In a minute," I responded. "You go ahead, I'll catch up."

TJ nodded his head and traipsed down the shore out of my sight. I looked fixedly at the moon. I withdrew the quartz from my pocket and placed it over my heart. A shooting star flashed across the sky.

"Keep him here with me," I chanted softly. Three

seconds later, the entire sky brightened. TJ rushed back to where I was in the spring.

"Whoa, what was that?" asked TJ. "Are you okay?"

I turned to him and smiled. "I'm fine. Are you ready to go?"

With a smile, TJ acknowledged that he was ready. He scratched his head. He was a bit shocked by my cheerfulness.

* * *

We maneuvered through the shadows and darkness of the night until we came upon the floating city. We crossed the bridge and met with Nylana at the entrance to the city. I handed her the rose quartz crystal.

"Just three more to go until we are free," said Nylana.

"We will bring them to you," I said.

"Good. I will show you your next vision tonight while you sleep." Nylana disappeared.

TJ and I walked to my grandma's cabin. It was late. The door creaked open as I tried to open it discreetly. Grandma was sound asleep on the couch. I tiptoed to my room and closed the door. I took a deep breath with my back against the door. TJ sat on my bed and buried his face in his hands.

I sat next to him. "So does Nylana know that once we retrieve all the crystals you'll become human?"

"Yeah, she is aware of the little arrangement God has set up for us." TJ spoke through his hands.

"School starts soon," I said.

"I know." TJ lifted his head up from his hands.

"Hey, if you, like, become human, we can hang out and go shopping together, like, all the time," I said.

"Hopefully I still can keep my powers, too."

"When we hang out, I won't feel awkward when people think I'm talking to myself," I said.

"Then people wouldn't avoid you, thinking you're loony toons," said TJ.

"Well, at least I'm embarrassing myself for an angel who protects me, gives me advice, who is always there for me, and makes me laugh." I leaned my head on his arm. He smoothed out my hair.

"You better get some rest, you little psychic." He kissed my forehead. "Goodnight, Jalissa." He tucked me into bed and reclaimed his position on the floor against the wall. My heavy eyes slowly shut as I drifted off to sleep.

Chapter 8

Imminent Premonition

I was engulfed in darkness. I couldn't see a thing. I was totally alone. I looked around frantically for TJ. I tripped and fell on my butt.

"TJ! Where are you?" I called out urgently. My eyes began to tear up. TJ appeared looking wan and bleary-eyed. His skin was pale and dull. He was taciturn. He seemed inanimate. I lifted myself from the ground and stopped crying.

"TJ?" I called out while approaching him. His expression was blank, devoid of his signature smile. He backed into the shadows.

"Hey, where are you going? Don't go! Wait!" I tried to grab him, but I only managed to grasp air. I felt lonely and cold. I didn't know what to do.

I awoke abruptly from my dream and clutched at my heart. I looked at my alarm clock and saw it was only midnight. I found TJ sitting up against the wall, sleeping. I let out a quick sigh of relief, laid back down, and stared at the ceiling.

"Did you have a nightmare?" TJ opened one of his eyes. I turned toward him.

"Yeah, I did. How did you know?" I asked.

"Your heart rate sped up, I could feel it. What was it about?" TJ asked.

"Well, I was alone, stranded in darkness. You were pale. I felt so disconnected from you. I reached out to you, but you disappeared." I rolled over and turned my back to him.

"That definitely wasn't a vision, because I'm not going anywhere," he said. I looked at him over my shoulder.

"I know," I said as if in a trance. "I'm going back to sleep to get the next crystal's location." But I was traumatized by what I'd seen. What if it was more than a dream?

I saw a town. It was the town near where my grandma goes. There was a small store. The store sign read "Wilson's Gifts." I explored inside the shop. I saw a dark hued man about grandma's age. He had a fuzzy, gray beard. His nametag read "Wilson." A metallic, silver crystal was mounted in a glass case. I assumed it was the crystal I needed to retrieve. A white flash interrupted my dream. I awakened. The sun's rays penetrated my eyelids. I sat up in my bed and stretched. TJ was still sleeping. I sat next to him and gently tapped him. He awakened gradually and began to stretch.

"Did you find it?" TJ asked, now fully alert.

"Yeah, but we need to go into town to retrieve it. It's mounted in a glass case inside a store." I tried to think of a way of getting there.

"Town is a ways from here. Maybe you can see if your grandma is going to town today," suggested TJ. "If she is, you can go with her and stop by the shop."

"All right, good idea. Let me go ask her." I went to look for my grandmother.

I found her cooking breakfast in the kitchen.

I sat next to her. "Hey, Grandma, are you going into town today?"

"Oh yes, dear, I have to get some groceries. Would you like to come with me?"

"Yes, I was hoping I could stop by Wilson's Gift store. I saw it when we were driving into town the other day."

"Oh yes, surely we could stop by. That would be wonderful. He's a good friend of mine. I've known him for ages. We went to school together years and years ago."

That was easier than expected. She was all for it. "Okay thanks, I'll go get ready." I scurried back to my room.

"So is she taking you?" asked TJ.

"Yep," I said. "I need to get ready, so give me a minute, okay?"

"Alright, let me know when you're ready." TJ disappeared.

I rushed to shower and wash my hair. I threw on a cute, yellow baby doll shirt and a pair of denim shorts. I pinned my hair up into a ponytail with bangs hanging down each side of my face. Once I was dressed, I checked to see if Grandma was ready to go. I walked in as she finished her breakfast.

"Come sit here and eat while I get ready to go." Grandma got up from the table. I finished eating in no time.

* * *

Grandma and I got into the car to go to town. Quietly, I called for TJ. He appeared.

"Aw, look at you girl," TJ said while snapping his fingers and flipping his wrist. "Looking all cute with your hair put up." I blushed a little.

We finally made it to town. Grandma parked the car in front of Mr. Wilson's shop. As we got out the car, I looked through the storefront window and saw Mr. Wilson wiping the counter. Grandma greeted Mr. Wilson while I sneaked off with TJ to search for the crystal. I found it. It was in a glass case in the corner of the store. We exchanged glances and hurried over to the case. A sign on the case read "Galena, stone of harmony." The words on the next line of the sign were more disconcerting. It read "Not for sale."

"Great," I said. "It's not even for sale."

"I would steal it, but I'm an angel," TJ said. "It's kind of bad for my rep."

How could he joke at a time like this?

"TJ, seriously, how are we going to get the crystal now?"

He seemed preoccupied. I saw him smiling as he looked back at Mr. Wilson and my grandmother. His lack of concern puzzled me.

"Is your grandmother single?" asked TJ with a devious grin.

"Yeah … wait a minute, where are you going with this?"

"Sheesh, Jalissa. I'm not trying to get with your granny. You're more my type. What about Wilson? Is he single?

"Yeah, I heard my grandma say his wife passed away a while back."

"Okay. Wilson plus granny equals crystal. Get it?" TJ nudged me.

"You think playing matchmaker will actually work?" I was doubtful.

We paid more attention to their conversation. They were giggling like giddy teenagers.

"Look at the way he's staring into your granny's eyes as she speaks," TJ said. "He is hypnotized, I tell you. We could snatch up the crystal now if we wanted to. His eyes are glued to her."

"Okay, okay. I see your point," I said. "How are we going to make this thing work, Einstein?"

TJ put his hand on his chin and thought of a plan.

"I got it!" he said. "Go over to your granny and show her how pretty the crystal is and tell her how nice it would be for you to have it."

I gave him a knowing look and walked over to where my grandmother and Mr. Wilson were talking.

"Hey grandma, look! This crystal is sooo pretty!" I clutched at my grandma's sleeve and pointed to the case.

"Oh, wow! It's beautiful. How much is it?" Grandma asked while searching the case for a price.

"Oh, um, that crystal isn't for sale," Mr. Wilson said. "Uh, but maybe we can trade something. I know you're from a Native American tribe. I'm sure you have plenty of antiques."

"Aw, that's a bummer. It really is beautiful." Grandma frowned.

"Okay, suggest they go on a date," TJ said.

"What?" I blurted.

"Just do it. It'll work."

I needed to get the crystal, so it was worth a shot.

"Maybe you guys can go on a date, you know, in

exchange for the crystal," I said. Mr. Wilson agreed immediately; Grandma's cheeks brightened to a cherry red. I was optimistic that TJ's plan might work.

"That would be a splendid idea," Grandma said, smiling at Mr. Wilson bashfully.

"How about we meet at Star Fall Field Park around eight tonight?" suggested Wilson. "I will have the galena crystal all polished and ready for you."

"All right, I'll see you later tonight," Grandma said. She exited the shop so excited that she nearly skipped to her car.

"Hey, you're good at this," I said to TJ.

"I am an angel, you know," said TJ.

* * *

We arrived back at the cabin. Grandma moved swiftly to the bathroom to get ready to go. Usually, Grandma was serene, but now she was extremely cheery. I shared a laugh with TJ, who was basking in my grandmother's jubilance.

"So how did you know Mr. Wilson and Grandma were interested in each other?" I asked. "I had no idea."

"I'm an angel," he said. "I'm sensitive to stuff like that. Also, it's the same way Wilson is feeling …" TJ paused. I looked at him curiously.

"Feeling what?" I asked.

"Let's watch them tonight in Star Fall Field Park." He was clearly trying to avoid the question.

"Um, okay." I played along with his attempted diversion.

Grandma walked into the living room. Her silky, dark, glistening hair was unbraided and hanging freely from her head. She wore a nice floral pink, white, and purple maxi dress with a white, netted shawl draped over her shoulders.

"How do I look?" she asked.

"You look stunning."

"All right, let's hope Mr. Wilson likes it as much as you do. I'll be back in a few hours. Will you be okay by yourself?"

"After all this time you been here with her, she finally decides to ask if you'll be okay by yourself," TJ said, shaking his head.

"Yes, I'll be fine." I sat on the couch and flipped through a magazine.

"I'll be back soon, sweetie." Grandma rushed over and kissed me good-bye. Then, she darted out of the door.

"It'll take us a little bit to get there, so we'll leave in five minutes," said TJ.

"Okay." I continued flipping through the magazine. Before my five minutes were up, I went to my room and grabbed a sweater.

* * *

It was vital that Mr. Wilson gave the crystal to my grandmother. The spirits *and TJ* depended on it.

We walked the dark path, depending on the glow of the half moon. The luminescent stars enveloped the night sky. I looked up to the sky, took a deep breath, and closed my eyes. A smile spread across my lips. When I opened my eyes, TJ was looking at me curiously.

"What are you smiling about?"

"I'm just enjoying the fresh air."

TJ spun around while he walked.

"It's pretty out here, just like someone I know. Not pointing fingers or anything." TJ pointed at me with his elbow as he pretended to stretch.

I chuckled at his silliness. "Thank you."

"Anytime, Jalissa," said TJ. "Oh! Look! There's Star Fall Field!" TJ pointed to an open plain bordered by trees. He motioned for me to follow him so we could hide behind a tree. Grandma and Mr. Wilson were sitting on the field on a picnic cloth.

"Aw, old couples look so cute."

"Hey, focus. Remember, we're here to see if he gives her the crystal."

"Oh yeah, let's watch." TJ directed his attention back to Grandma and Mr. Wilson.

As they conversed, Grandma seemed to be in a trance. She couldn't take her eyes off of him. It was kind of scary. Wilson reached into his coat pocket and withdrew the galena crystal and handed it to my grandma. She smiled, said something, and put it in her purse. We were too far away, so I couldn't hear what they were saying.

"Ha! We got the crystal, all thanks to me!" TJ said, relishing in the success of his plan.

"And me too! It's my grandma and my gift to interact with spirits," I said, pouting.

"Okay, okay. This isn't No Child Left Behind. Thank you, Jalissa, for helping me and freeing the spirits. I know you didn't have to if you didn't want to." He actually sounded sincere when he said it.

"Aw, you're welcome," I said. "I'd do anything for my best friend."

With the crystal safely back in Grandma's possession, I knew it was time to move to the next phase. "All right, let's head back to the cabin so I can find out where the next crystal is located."

TJ agreed and we headed back to the cabin.

"Just two more crystals to go, you know."

"Yeah, I know," TJ said.

"Hey, cheer up! We'll have given all the crystals to Nylana before I leave to go back to school. You can count on me!" I tried to imitate TJ's cheerfulness.

"Hey, that almost sounds like me," he said.

We finally made it back to the cabin.

"We will have to wait until tomorrow for your

grandma to give you the crystal. Until then, you can go nighty night, and maybe Nylana will show you the next one."

"Sounds like a plan. I'll see you in the morning."

I took a quick shower and washed my hair. I slipped into my pajamas and plopped down on the bed. Just two more crystals to retrieve. The spirits would be freed and TJ would become human.

Chapter 9

Paranormal Corruption

I felt the sun's rays piercing my eyelids. I slowly opened my eyes and realized it was morning. I hadn't had a vision. I was distraught. I checked the wall for TJ, but he was not in his usual resting place. I frantically whispered his name, trying to summon him, and just when I was really about to freak out, I heard his voice.

"I'm right here. What's up?" He was cool, calm, and collected. The total opposite of how I felt at that moment.

"I … I … I didn't have a vision," I stammered.

"What? Okay," he said, "let's go pay Nylana a visit."

"All right," I said. "Let me go get dressed and get the galena crystal from my grandmother."

TJ disappeared. I showered and hurriedly dressed in a white, v-neck T-shirt and black shorts. I heard Grandma's voice, so I rushed into the kitchen and found her talking on the telephone.

"All right, I will stop bye later, okay. Bye." I waited for her to hang up the phone before I entered the kitchen.

"How was the date last night?" I asked, settling down and casually pouring myself a glass of orange juice.

"Oh sweetie, it was wonderful. Here, I got that crystal you wanted. Thanks a lot for your help, Jalissa. I really do like that Mr. Wilson." The mere mention of his name made her smile.

"I'm glad you do, and thanks for getting the crystal for me." If she only knew how much it really meant to me.

"You are very welcome." She kissed me on the forehead. "I need to go run some errands. I'll be back in a few." She grabbed a bagel and left.

"Are you ready to go?" asked TJ.

"Yeah, I'm ready," I said. "Let's go to the lake and speak with Nylana."

* * *

We maneuvered through the forest hastily. The trees seemed to be plotting against us, because we fought through branches all the way to the lake. To our dismay, the floating city wasn't there. I took the galena crystal from my pocket and held it up to the sky. Nothing happened. I looked back at TJ frantically, but before I could completely panic, Nylana appeared on the shore.

"I didn't have a vision last night."

"Yes, I am aware of that. Your assistance is no longer needed."

"What do you mean?" I asked, gasping. "I have two more crystals to retrieve." I started pacing back and forth.

"The sea spirit demands that we stay here on earth."

"What about TJ?" I was furious.

"I'm sorry, but there is nothing we can do," explained Nylana. "We must obey the sea spirit or be condemned."

"Thanks a lot for your help," I said sarcastically. "I'll talk to the sea spirit myself!" I kicked sand into the lake and stomped off into the forest. TJ ran after me. Not really sure of what I'd do when I got there, I ran toward the ocean. After my anger subsided and my adrenaline waned, I realized I was exhausted. I stopped and rested on a log in the forest. TJ caught up to me and sat next to me in silence.

"What are we going to do now?" TJ asked.

"I'm going to talk to the sea spirit myself. That's not fair, TJ," I said. "You guys had a deal. It's not fair!"

TJ grabbed my hand softly and rubbed it. "Everything's going to be okay." He smiled, radiating peace. I stared at him in confusion.

"Why are you so calm? You might not be able to become human!" I said.

Softly, he said, "I know."

"I'm not just going to let you stand here and be

deceived like that," I snapped as I sprang up from the log. With anger-filled determination, I walked toward the ocean. TJ smiled and followed after me. We finally reached the ocean's shore. The waves were gentle. I braced myself and took a deep breath.

"Hey, sea spirit!" I yelled.

"Jalissa, what are you doing?" TJ asked, concerned.

"What do you think I'm doing?" I snapped. "I'm trying to summon the sea spirit."

The winds began to gust. The waves crashed against the shore. The clouds darkened and became denser. TJ grabbed me and wrapped his arms around me.

"Jalissa, let's go! These are spirits, not people. You can't talk to them like that!" He pulled me away from the water.

"Yes, I can!" I wrested away from his grasp and ran back to the shore. Five water spouts formed in the ocean.

"Jalissa, get back!" Before I could take another step, a white bubble engulfed me. "I put a shield around you! Just stay back!" TJ ran toward the water. His eyes glowed lustrously. I was astonished by what I saw. The twisters thrust toward the shore. TJ spread his arms wide and clapped his hands together forcefully. Radiant beams of light shot from the sky and pierced the twisters. The twisters disintegrated. Violent strikes of lightning flashed throughout the sky. A flash of lighting struck the sand. A white, shapeless figure appeared from the dust of the strike's aftermath. It flowed like an amoeba of water as it hovered just above the beach.

"I am the sea spirit. Who dares disturb my slumber?" she boomed in an irritated tone.

"I do!" I shouted from inside my protective bubble.

"Silence human! Don't say anything you will regret!" the sea spirit roared.

"Don't talk to her like that!" TJ yelled at the sea spirit.

"Angel, shall you dare defile the precepts of the universe?" the sea spirit questioned, sharpening her tone.

"Look here, we had a deal!" said TJ. "I helped Jalissa free the spirits. Now I should become human. You came up short on your end of the bargain!"

"Angel, the universe doesn't bargain. You are fortunate that we sometimes show mercy. It is an eternal cycle. You either accept it or perish!" The sea spirit's command sounded ruthless.

"No! Your cycle is stupid! Things will be fair!" TJ shook his fist in defiance. He pounded his fist into the ground. An enormous explosion of light illuminated the sky. I was blinded by the brightness. After the light faded, TJ stood alone like a Spartan statue. His breathing was heavy. The sea spirit was nowhere in sight. My shield dissipated. I got up and walked over to TJ.

"I vanquished the sea spirit. I'm tired of the false hope that shapes our universe. I didn't like how she was talking to you. She talked to you as if you were nothing; you are something. I'm tired of people being controlled." His words were drenched with frustration.

"TJ …" I said softly.

"You aren't a puppet. You're an actual human being."

"TJ, what will happen to you? You destroyed a force of nature."

"Don't worry, I am a force of nature," TJ said. "I also work very closely with God. The worst they could do is put me up for retention."

"No, not that!" The mere thought of losing TJ sounded dreadful. I ran to him and swallowed him in my arms.

"I will be fine, don't worry," he reassured me.

* * *

A transparent stairway materialized near where we stood on the beach. It extended from the shore far up into the clouds.

"TJ and Jalissa," a voice summoned from above, "come forth and face thy God."

TJ turned to me.

"God summons us," he said. "We must go up the stairway to see him. Hold my hand."

I nodded, and we ascended the celestial stairway. The density of the clouds lessened and revealed a colossal golden gate. TJ pushed it open.

"Come forth to mine altar," a powerful yet peaceful voice commanded. We stepped onto a high platform. Three hooded entities in white cloaks surrounded us— one stood behind us while the other two flanked us on either side. We were on trial.

Standing in front of God was nothing like I had imagined. He was a white-silhouetted, male-looking entity wielding a long staff.

"We have called forth to thee subsequent to the extermination of the sea spirit," God said. His voice was marked with duality. It was stern yet genial.

TJ braced himself and spoke.

"We had an agreement," TJ said. "If I helped Jalissa free the spirits, then I would be able to become human."

"Yes, I do have recollection of that arrangement. Go on."

"The sea spirit commanded Nylana to remain on earth, which restricted us from retrieving the remaining crystals to free the spirits. We decided to confront the sea spirit regarding the alteration of the proposal." I was amazed at how confidently he spoke, given the circumstances and the audience. "The sea spirit threatened Jalissa with her powers and tried to harm her. My job is to protect Jalissa, and that is why I annihilated the sea spirit."

"I understand," God said. "However, the cycle of life must continue, and I must replace the sea spirit. You defiled a timeless precept of the universe. I must suspend you."

"What? No!" I said. I may have spoken out of turn, but God couldn't suspend TJ—he just couldn't.

God turned to me. "I will assign another angel in his place."

"No, I don't want another angel watching over me. Only him. If not TJ, then none at all."

"So be it," God said. "You will be without an angel. You, TJ, must remain in the heavens." God ordered the three, cloaked entities to escort me back to earth. I hurriedly embraced TJ.

"Please don't let them take me," I said, squeezing him tighter.

"I will come back for you, don't worry," TJ said. His smile was reassuring although not completely convincing.

"Stop smiling," I whimpered. "I hate this."

"You'll be okay. You're strong."

The hooded entities intervened and escorted me back to my grandmother's cabin. For the first time since I met TJ, I was totally alone. It felt like something was missing, knowing he wasn't here with me. I called his name countless times, but he never came.

It was so unfair. I tried to make sense of the mess that had taken over my emotions. I needed someone to blame. It was my fault. I did speak to the sea spirit disrespectfully. No, it was the sea spirit's fault. She shouldn't have attacked me. Then TJ wouldn't have had to protect me. I guess TJ didn't have to destroy the sea spirit either. He had issues with the cycle of the universe, so he overreacted out of frustration.

The incident caused me to resent life. I contemplated the purpose of my existence. I felt like a puppet, and the universe was my puppeteer.

* * *

To deal with my dark emotions about the world, I started keeping diaries and writing poems. I spent lots of time locked away in my room lying in bed staring at the ceiling.

A car parked outside. I didn't bother to peek out of the window to see who it was. It wasn't TJ, so I didn't care. My bedroom door opened. My mother stood in my doorway. I was so entangled in the emotions of my secret life with TJ that I forgot school was coming up. My mother had decided to pick me up a few days early.

"I know I'm a bit early, so I'll give you some time to get ready to go. I'll be out in the car," she said. She left my room and looked through the house for her mother. I overheard them talking about me.

"She's seems a little disappointed; she must've had a blast here," my mother said, sounding somewhat surprised.

"I guess she did," acknowledged Grandma. "She can always come to visit next summer."

I tuned out the rest of what they were saying. I did have fun here, but I had all my fun with TJ. His suspension took him away from me. That's what caused my disappointment.

I dragged my stuff and myself into the car and plugged my earphones in my ears. I rode home without TJ.

Chapter 10

Pleasant Reunion

"Honey, are you ready to go?" my mom shouted from the kitchen. I searched my room for my diary and stuffed it in my bag.

"Yes, I'm coming. I was looking for my diary."

"Hmm, you never really liked diaries before," my mom said. "Why the change of heart?"

"Well, it's a good way to vent my frustrations about how things are in the world, and it's a good way to deal with my boredom." Things hadn't been the same since last summer.

"Okay, kiddo, well, let's get going." My mom went outside to get into the car. I moped out of the house shortly afterward. We were on our way once again to my grandmother's cabin. Staring out of the window, I reminisced about last summer. Just a year ago, we drove the same route, but TJ was here to pester me in the backseat. I really missed him, but there was nothing I could do about it.

When we arrived at my grandmother's cabin, she was standing in the driveway. I smiled and waved at her from the car. When I got out, she greeted me with hugs and kisses like always. As I took my stuff into my room, I passed Mr. Wilson sitting in the living room with his niece, Ayala, who was visiting from Cameroon, Africa. I greeted them and continued on to my room to unpack my belongings. I looked out the window toward the lake. I picked up my diary and a pen and went out to the lake for inspiration in my writing. I left the cabin through the back door, avoiding Grandma and her cheerful company. I just wanted to be alone. When I reached the lake, I sat at the spot on the cliff where I pushed TJ over the edge. I opened my diary and sat there. I was too preoccupied to write. I placed my diary on the ground and took a deep breath. I arose from the ground and closed my eyes.

"TJ," I said.

I opened my eyes hopefully, but he wasn't there. I frowned. I wasn't surprised he didn't show. I'd called his name every day since he'd left. A feeling of hopelessness began to build inside of me. I fell to the ground and buried my face in my hands disappointedly.

"Miss me?" I heard a familiar male voice. I slowly lifted my head in disbelief. It was TJ. He was back. A huge smile covered my face. I darted over to him and embraced him in a bear hug.

"Oh my god, I missed you so much," I said. "I was so lonely and bored without you and your sarcastic and funny remarks!"

"Hey, he's my God, too," he said. "Aw, I missed you, too. I'm finally off of punishment."

"You haven't change a bit."

"I swear I thought about you all this time. I could hear you calling my name every day. I couldn't go to see you, but at least I knew you were okay. Once God proclaimed that my punishment had ended, I dove straight from the sky to see you. Literally."

"Really?"

"Yeah, I sure did. Hey, what's that?" TJ asked. "You didn't have a diary before. Can I see it?"

"Oh yeah, here," I said. "It's just about my emotions during your absence."

TJ stared at it and raised his eyebrows. He began to open it.

"Hey no! Don't read it!" I attempted to take it back from him. He held it up over his head, out of my reach. I jumped up and tried to grasp it. He relented and handed it to me.

"I'm not human, remember," he said. "I already read it by staring at it."

"Oh …" I held on to the diary tightly, slightly embarrassed. TJ stared at me and smiled. He fixed a flyaway in my hair by moving it behind my ear.

"I really am glad to see you. I got my job back. Yay!"

"Oh, look! What's that shiny thing in the water?" I pointed down from the cliff. TJ ran up to the edge and peered around. I crept up behind him.

"I think it's a crystal," TJ said.

"Really?" I was astonished. I just wanted him close to the edge so I could push him off the cliff again. I ran up beside him on the cliff. He picked me up and jumped into the water. I surfaced laughing.

"Hey, you cheated! I was supposed to push you in the water."

"It was my turn." TJ backstroked in the water. I grinned at him.

"Let's head back to my grandma's place. I need to put my diary up so it's safe."

"All right."

We dried off and headed to my grandma's cabin.

* * *

My grandmother greeted me at the door with Penela standing next to her.

"Look, sweetie, look who's here to visit you!"

"Hey, Penela, how are you doing?"

"I'm fine," Penela said. "I heard you were in town, so I came by to see how you were doing. Do you want to take a walk with me? It's kind of noisy in here with all the company." Penela must have just wanted to talk to me privately. Grandma, Wilson, and Ayala were the only people in the cabin, and they were not being loud.

"Yeah, sure." I walked outside with her. It was twilight. My mind drifted as we walked. For a whole year, I was without TJ. Now he was back, and he came back for me.

"Jalissa, are you okay?" Penela startled me. I didn't realize she had been speaking to me that whole time.

"Uh, I'm fine, I was just—"

"Daydreaming," Penela answered for me.

"Yeah, pretty much." I scratched my head in embarrassment.

"So, Jalissa, do you like anyone?" That was a random question.

"Well, yes. He's someone special." I twisted my hands bashfully.

"C'mon, spit it out," Penela said.

"You shouldn't tell her." TJ walked up beside me.

"Why not?"

"Why not what?" Penela gave me a puzzled look. I forgot she was in my presence.

"Oh, it's nothing." I was embarrassed.

"Because she won't believe you. She'll think you're loony tunes," TJ said.

"Ha ha, very funny." I did it again.

"Um, Earth to Jalissa," Penela said. "Nobody is here except for you and me."

"I'm here. Duh!" said TJ. "See, she already thinks you're crazy."

"Penela, do you think I'm crazy?" I asked.

"Well, I don't know," she said. "You *are* talking to yourself."

"My mind is just so full right now," I explained.

"She has no idea," interjected TJ.

"Do you have an imaginary friend?" Penela asked.

"You can kind of say that." I smiled at her nervously. TJ raised his eyebrows up and down playfully.

"Don't worry, I won't judge you," Penela reassured me.

"Thanks," I replied. Penela and I found a spot in the grass and lay there. We looked up to the stars on this dark Friday night.

"The stars are so beautiful." TJ said as he lay down next to me.

"Yeah, they are."

"What is?" Penela asked.

"Nothing." I continued to gaze up at the stars.

"You know, I wish I could be human so everybody wouldn't think you were crazy," TJ said.

"Aw, how considerate of you," I said aloud.

"Um, I didn't do anything considerate." Penela gave me a puzzled stare. "Well, I'm 'bout to take a nap right here. You go 'head and continue talking to whoever you're talking to." She closed her eyes.

"Oh no! You bored your friend by talking to me," TJ said. I looked at him, then rolled my eyes and laughed.

"Why are *you* laughing?"

"It's just you're hilarious. You always have something funny to say."

"You just now noticed that?"

"Of course not," I said. "I just had a lot of time to reflect while you were on restriction."

"TJ, why did we meet?" I was still curious.

"It's complicated and confusing."

"Well, tell me anyway." I rolled over and stared into his glistening, celestial eyes. He stared at the sky for a moment and took a deep breath.

"Well, let's just say God said it was our time to meet, because I serve a purpose for you."

"So what's your purpose?" I ruffled his light brown hair.

"My purpose is God's will for you." He remarked cleverly. "Maybe you should wake your friend up. She's beginning to snore." TJ pointed toward Penela.

"Hmm, your right," I said, grinning. "It's getting late. I better get her up."

"I don't want to interrupt your conversation any longer," TJ said. "I guess I better go. Just call me if you need me. I'll be there in a heartbeat. I promise." TJ faded in the dim light. "You know I'm always watching over you."

"Bye TJ. I'll see you tomorrow," I said, then I tapped on Penela's shoulder.

* * *

"Huh!" Penela said in her sleep. "Wha! I didn't take the cookies grandma! I swear!"

I wondered what she was dreaming about. "Oh, Jalissa?" she said as she woke up. "It's late." She stared at her watch.

"Yeah, we should start walking back."

"So what were you doing the whole time I was asleep?"

"You really, honestly want to know what I was doing while you were asleep?"

"Yes."

"Penela, this may sound crazy but …"

"But what?" she asked.

"I was talking to an angel," I said. "My best friend is an angel. There, I said it."

"What? Really?"

I was shocked. What I said didn't seem to freak her out at all. She seemed more curious than anything else.

"I talk to an angel! That's why when you talk to me, I seem distracted. Because I am!"

TJ appeared. "Hey, I heard you yelling. I came to check on you."   "Wow, who is she? I want to meet her!" Penela was excited about the prospects of meeting an angel.

"That's odd. I thought she would be startled to know you talked to an angel." TJ rolled his eyes. "Also, I find it very insulting to be labeled as a female."

Penela asked me question after question. She was captivated by my story.

"Well, my angel is a guy, and his name is TJ."

"Oh, sorry TJ," apologized Penela as she looked around for TJ. "Is he here now? What does he look like? Can he see me? Is he cute?"

"If only she could see me," TJ said cockily nodding his head.

"Oh! I get it now! Is he that special someone you like? Hmm? Hmm?" Penela said, swinging my arms playfully.

"Huh?" I blushed until my face was cherry red. TJ watched in awe. Butterflies twisted my stomach into knots. I felt paralyzed. TJ's face lit up. I mean, I had feelings for him but …

At that moment, I was overwhelmed by a special connection with TJ that I had previously suppressed. My heart beat faster and faster as I stared at him. Blood rushed throughout my body so rapidly that my skin tingled. *Could it be? Did I love my best friend? Did I love an angel?* Memories of us together came back to me in droves. I snapped back to reality.

Penela and TJ watched me silently. I felt claustro-phobic. I felt so trapped. I felt like all my emotions were about to erupt. I didn't know what to do. My eyes watered, and I felt tears roll down my cheeks. I couldn't contain it anymore. I let it all out. I sobbed profusely.

"Don't cry, Jalissa. I love you. I love you with all my heart. That is my purpose. My purpose is to be here for you, watch over you, and love you always."

"Is that TJ?" Penela asked, pointing at TJ in awe.

"You can see him?" I asked.

"Clearly!"

I ran to TJ and held him in my arms.

"TJ, I loved you, I just didn't know …"

"You know all the times, all the hints I tried to give you," he said. "I love you way beyond your imagination." He pulled me closer. "I think about you twenty-four seven, every day, all day. I am always happy when I see you."

"This is beautiful," Penela said, shedding tears of joy.

"It feels really good to hold you like this," I said. "This is amazing. You're human now."

"I'm glad to be with you," TJ said. "I promise I will always stay by your side. I promise." TJ embraced me tighter.

I sobbed. I sobbed because I was happy. Tears of joy coated my face. I had never felt such a beautiful feeling in my entire life.

"What's that?" Penela pointed into the sky.

A note dropped from the sky and landed between TJ and me. I opened the letter and read it.

Dear Jalissa,

I have handed you a wonderful gift. A gift many would die to have. The kind of gift that seems impossible. This gift is extremely rare and is made especially for you. I hope you enjoy the gift that will last you a lifetime. It is true love.

Love always,
God

P.S. He's just serving his purpose.